W9-ASC-274

Girls Got Game

girls' SOFTBALL

Winning on the Diamond

by Heather E. Schwartz

Consultant
Bill Plummer III
National Softball Hall of Fame Manager
Amateur Softball Association

Capstone
press®

Mankato, Minnesota

Snap Books are published by Capstone Press,
151 Good Counsel Drive, P.O. Box 669, Mankato, Minnesota 56002.
www.capstonepress.com

Library of Congress Cataloging-in-Publication Data
Schwartz, Heather E.
    Girls' softball : winning on the diamond / by Heather E. Schwartz.
    p. cm.—(Snap books. Girls got game)
    Summary: "Describes softball, the skills needed for it, and ways
to compete"—Provided by publisher.
    Includes bibliographical references and index.
    ISBN-13: 978-0-7368-6824-2 (hardcover)
    ISBN-10: 0-7368-6824-0 (hardcover)
    ISBN-13: 978-0-7368-9929-1 (softcover pbk.)
    ISBN-10: 0-7368-9929-4 (softcover pbk.)
    1. Softball for women—Juvenile literature. I. Title. II. Series.
GV881.3.S35 2007
796.357'8—dc22   2006021505

Editor: Becky Viaene
Designer: Bobbi J. Wyss
Illustrator: Kyle Grenz
Photo Researcher: Charlene Deyle

Photo Credits: Capstone Press/Karon Dubke, 5, 7, 8–9, 10, 12–13, 14–15,
17, 18, 21, 23; Comstock, 6 (softball), 7 (mitt), 22; Comstock Klips, cover;
Corbis/Reuters/Mike Finn-Kelcey, 25; Getty Images Inc./Andy Lyons, 29;
Getty Images Inc./Donald Miralle, 28; Getty Images Inc./Ezra Shaw, 27;
Getty Images Inc./Guang Niu, cover; Getty Images Inc./Matthew Stockman,
26; Hot Shots Photo, 32; iStockphoto Inc./Rob Geddes, 8; Shutterstock/Lori
Carpenter, 19

1 2 3 4 5 6 12 11 10 09 08 07

TABLE OF CONTENTS

CHAPTER ONE

PLAY BALL

Has anyone ever told you that you run, throw, hit, or catch like a girl? Guess what—that's great! Comments like those are compliments. After all, some of the best softball players, like Jennie Finch, Lisa Fernandez, and Dot Richardson, are women. Maybe you've wished you could play softball like these fabulous athletes. Who knows? Someday you might.

Even if you've never played softball, you can learn the skills you'll need to know. With practice, you may even make it all the way to a professional team someday.

So What Is Softball Anyway?

Watch a game and you can't help but notice—softball is similar to baseball. Both games are played on a diamond-shaped field, with bases and players in the same positions. One team is the offense and sends players up to bat. The other team is the defense. Defense works in the field to stop batters from scoring runs.

Softball isn't exactly like baseball, though. For softball, you'll use some different equipment, including a larger ball and a metal bat, instead of a wood one. You also can choose between playing slow-pitch or fast-pitch softball. In slow-pitch, the ball is thrown with an arc, so it travels slowly. In fast-pitch, the ball travels in a straight line and moves quickly toward the batter.

Get in Gear

A glove protects your hand and helps you catch. Mitts have more padding than gloves and are usually worn by catchers and first base players. Another important part of your uniform is a helmet. Helmets protect batters and runners from being hit by the ball.

Keeping Score

Playing in the field is fun, but you want your team up to bat as much as possible. That's the only time you can score. When you play softball, you're part of a team with a common goal: victory!

A softball game has seven innings—meaning seven chances for each team to bat. Players score by running around the bases all the way back to home plate. Your team keeps batting until the opposing team makes three outs.

Staying on the Sand

Want to test your softball skills? Head to first base. This position is usually action-packed. A **first base player** must have excellent catching and throwing skills. You'll need to quickly grab balls thrown your way and tag runners for an out.

You need to be speedy to cover second base. Fast feet help **second base players** move to catch fly balls, grounders, and throws from outfielders and the catcher. They also use their quick hands to tag out runners.

Third base players need to be good at guarding the base and the baseline. They also need to be ready to catch and quickly throw to home or first base.

"She's OUT!"

Three outs end the batting team's chance to score. Here's how you can get a player out:

- Catch a ball that's been hit before it touches the ground.

- Touch a runner with the ball while she's between bases.

- With the ball in your glove, step on the base before the runner can get there.

A pitcher can also get outs by sending three good pitches, called strikes, that a batter doesn't hit.

"The team with the best athletes doesn't usually win. It's the team with the athletes who play best together."

—Lisa Fernandez,
U.S. softball pitcher and
three-time Olympic gold medalist

Outfield

Are you good at catching fly balls? Can you throw fast and far? Then get ready to move from the sandy infield to the grassy outfield.

In the outfield, it's your job to move the ball back to the infield—fast and with accuracy. All outfielders need to be able to determine where the ball, especially fly balls, will land. But certain skills make some players better at certain positions.

Since more batters are right-handed, they tend to hit toward left field. Besides catching, **left fielders** must be able to throw to the third base player with power and speed.

If you can run fast, then center field is the position for you. **Center fielders** run quickly to cover one of the largest areas of the field. They're ready to catch a ball to their right or left. They use their strong arms to throw to the second base player or to the shortstop.

Throwing is one of the most important skills needed to be a great **right fielder**. Right fielders use their strong arms and good aim to throw the ball to first base. Sometimes they even need to throw all the way across the field to third base. Right fielders also need to be ready to catch any balls that the first base player misses.

Want to play both infield and outfield? **Short fielder** is the position for you. Located between the second base player and center fielder, short fielders need to be ready to catch. Also called a rover, this position is used only in slow-pitch softball.

CHAPTER THREE

GET IN THE GAME

Feel like a game of softball? All you have to do is join a city or school softball team. These teams play other teams from nearby cities. So sign up and start playing with other girls who live in your community.

Get to know a teammate better by asking her to play catch with you. Start by throwing directly to each other. Then work on more difficult moves. Roll the ball along the ground to practice catching grounders. Toss the ball high in the air to work on catching fly balls.

"The greatest legacy that I could leave would be one of inspiring others to realize that they have been given unbelievable talent, that they are able to accomplish whatever they are willing to work hard for."

—Dot Richardson, former U.S. Women's National Softball Team second base player

Getting Better

Batting, throwing, and catching. You love them all. But how can you become better at them quickly? By attending softball clinics. Clinics are one-day minicamps. You can also improve your game by attending a week-long softball camp. You'll spend four to six hours on the field each day. Who wouldn't learn a few new skills with that schedule?

Swinging Toward Success

Need some practice to hit that home run? At automated batting cages, a machine pitches to you. Or you can use a batting tee, which will hold the ball so you can hit. But one of best ways to practice batting is to have a teammate pitch to you. No matter how you practice, you're bound to become a better batter.

CHAPTER FOUR

BECOMING THE BEST

Training to become an excellent softball player starts before you even reach the field. Getting enough sleep, stretching, exercising, and eating healthy help you prepare to play your best.

To be at the top of your game, you should have 8 to 9 hours of sleep each night. Getting the right amount of sleep lowers your risk of injuries and helps you feel great.

Stretching also helps prevent injuries. Get your muscles ready to work out by stretching for 10 to 15 minutes. Hold each stretch about 20 to 30 seconds.

Want to run around the bases quicker and throw farther? You can gain strength in your arms and legs by exercising them. Sprinting and lifting weights will help you improve your game.

Fueling Your Body:

Just like a car can't run without gas, your body can't run well without healthy foods. Here are some healthy, high-energy foods to eat 2 hours before exercising:

- Cereal
- Fruit
- Vegetables
- Fish
- Nuts
- Yogurt

Your body needs water too. Drink at least 2 cups, 1 to 2 hours before exercising.

Getting in the Club

Play on a city or school softball team for awhile and you'll probably be pretty good. Ready for the next step?

Join a club team. They travel to other communities and play more competitively. To get on a club team, you'll need to try out. Trying out means catching, throwing, and batting while a coach judges your every move. It may sound a little scary, but don't worry. Just do your best and try to impress the coaches.

"There is always room for improvement. Push yourself to the max, or you'll never know just how good you can be!

—Jennie Finch,
U.S. National Women's Softball Team Pitcher

The Big Leagues

If you practice hard, and are good enough, you can play softball for your high school and college teams. As a college senior, you could be picked by one of the seven National Pro Fastpitch (NPF) teams to play professionally. Players try out or they're selected from colleges all over the country.

The U.S. Women's National Softball Team holds tryouts, too. Making the team is difficult. If you get on the national team, you'll be part of major international events. From competing in the International Softball Federation (ISF) World Championships to the Olympics, you'll be working hard.

On the U.S. Women's National Softball Team:

- Pitchers throw the ball at a speed of 60 to 63 miles (97 to 101 kilometers) per hour. That's as fast as a car driving down the highway!
- Infielders and outfielders have a throwing speed of 50 miles (80 kilometers) per hour.

2004 U.S. National Team

CHAPTER FIVE

PRO PLAYERS

As these players know, it takes a winning attitude to make it big on the ball field. Here's how they did it—and how you can too.

Take it from outstanding center fielder Laura Berg–practice pays. She said that without practice and a stick-to-it attitude she never would have made it to the Olympics. Berg's practice and attitude helped her team win gold medals in the 1996, 2000, and 2004 Olympics.

Laura Berg

Lisa Fernandez

Lisa Fernandez's first competitive game as pitcher was a flop. But Fernandez's hard work helped her be known today for her ability to strike out batters. Over the years, she followed her motto of never being satisfied and kept improving her skills. Today Fernandez is a three-time Olympic gold medalist. She says, "A true champion is someone that works hard, is dedicated and sacrifices. Not only on the field, but off the field, not only if you win, but if you lose."

Practice has paid off for Jennie Finch. Batters pay attention when her drop ball, rise ball, curveball, screwball, or changeup pitches come whizzing by. Today, Finch's top pitching speed is 71 miles (114 kilometers) per hour. She's also an Olympic gold medalist. Along with practice, Finch's positive attitude and focus on teamwork have helped her become an outstanding athlete. She says, "I do my job at the mound, and then I do my job at the plate, always working on helping the team any way I can. Never limit yourself, never be satisfied, and smile—it's free!"

USA

Jennie Finch

When Dot Richardson was a kid in the 1960s, softball was considered a boys' sport. Her attitude? Whatever! She grew up to hit the winning home run at the 1996 Olympics. Richardson retired after winning another gold medal in the 2000 Olympics. Off the field, Richardson also inspired girls by becoming an orthopedic surgeon at a time when few women were doctors.

Dot Richardson

Want to be known for your amazing athletic abilities? If you're working to improve your softball skills, you're definitely on the right track. Keep at it. You'll have a success story of your own to tell one day.

GLOSSARY

defense (DI-fenss)—the team that is trying to stop runs from being scored

fly ball (FLY BALL)—a ball hit into the air

infield (IN-feeld)—the area of a softball field that includes first, second, and third bases, and home plate

inning (IN-ing)—a part of a softball game when players on each team get a turn batting; softball has seven innings.

offense (aw-FENSS)—the team that is trying to score runs; in softball the offense is the team that is batting.

out (OUT)—when a base runner must leave the field because they weren't able to reach the base before the ball

outfield (OUT-feeld)—the grassy area beyond where the bases are placed

FAST FACTS

Softball and baseball were once for boys only. Those rules were revised in 1974. The Amateur Softball Association (ASA) now registers over 1.2 million girls on youth fast-pitch teams in the U.S. each year.

The ASA Hall of Fame is located in Oklahoma City, Oklahoma. So far, the hall members include 52 women fast-pitch players and 9 slow-pitch players.

Women's softball was finally added to the Olympics in 1996. The U.S. Women's National Softball Team was ready. They won gold medals in 1996, 2000, and 2004. Now that's a winning team!

READ MORE

Brill, Marlene Targ. *Winning Women in Baseball and Softball.* Sports Success. Hauppauge, N.Y.: Barron's, 2000.

Lockman, Darcy. *Softball For Fun!* Sports for Fun! Minneapolis: Compass Point Books, 2006.

Nitz, Kristin Wolden. *Play-by-Play. Softball.* Minneapolis: Lerner, 2000.

INTERNET SITES

FactHound offers a safe, fun way to find Internet sites related to this book. All of the sites on FactHound have been researched by our staff.

Here's how:

1. Visit *www.facthound.com*

2. Choose your grade level.

3. Type in this book ID **0736868240** for age-appropriate sites. You may also browse subjects by clicking on letters, or by clicking on pictures and words.

4. Click on the **Fetch It** button.

Facthound will fetch the best sites for you!

ABOUT THE AUTHOR

Growing up in upstate New York, Heather E. Schwartz always dreamed of playing softball in the big leagues. Although she never played professionally, she always enjoyed a good backyard ball game.

These days, Heather works as a freelance writer for kid-friendly publications, such as *National Geographic Kids*. She especially likes working on articles about sports, fitness, and health. She also teaches workshops for girls through Girls Inc., a national non-profit youth organization.

INDEX